BAA BAA TOM SHEEP

MO

BUZZ

SNICKER

RIFF

WHEEZY

FARMER FI

THE SHEEP

WACK

BACH

THE HENS

PURDEY

REV

TOM

WINNIE

MATT

First published in Great Britain by HarperCollins Children's Books in 2004

3 5 7 9 10 8 6 4 2

ISBN: 0-00-718902-8

Text adopted from the original script by Mark Holloway

The Contender Entertainment Group
48 Margaret Street, London W1W 8SE

Tractor Tom © Contender Ltd 2002

BAA BAA TOM SHEEP

Collins

An imprint of HarperCollins*Publishers*

It was lambing time at Springhill Farm. Tom and Fi had come to feed the sheep. But the sheep were nowhere to be found.

"Where have they gone?" asked Fi.
Someone had left the gate open. Riff and Fi went to find out where the sheep were.

Matt was busy loading up Rev and Buzz with honey and flour.

Suddenly, his mobile phone rang. It was Fi asking him to look for the sheep.

When Matt left, Rev and Buzz, who were feeling naughty, decided to have a race!

Ready, steady, go!

They raced out of the farm. Tom was waiting for Fi beside the bridge.

As Buzz flew over the bridge the honey jars fell off his carrier and smashed all over Tom!

Then, as Rev raced over the bridge, the bag of flour bounced out of his carrier and that went all over Tom too!

Now Tom was white all over!

Tom was still covered in flour when a little lamb came by.

"Ma-ma!" said the lamb.

Just then, Fi and Riff returned.

Fi spotted the lamb and decided to take her back to the farm to get her some milk. But the little lamb wouldn't drink. She kept trying to go back to Tom.

Then Matt and Fi had a brilliant idea. They tied a bottle of milk to the front of Tom! Soon the lamb was happily drinking the milk.

"She thinks that Tom is her mummy," said Fi. "But we need to find her real mother."

Matt offered to help. "I'll do that," he said. "I'm good with sheep."

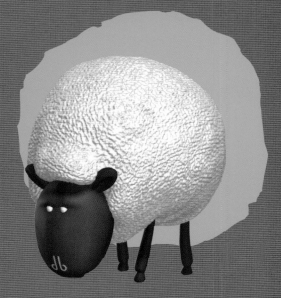

Wherever Tom went that day the little lamb was sure to go. She even tried to help Tom plough the field by pulling a stick in her mouth.

No matter how hard Matt tried he couldn't get the little lamb to stay in the field with the other sheep.

Matt even tried to show the lamb how to act like a sheep.

"You are a lamb, not a tractor," he said. "You eat grass, you do little lamby jumps in the air, and you drink water from the river," he explained, as he walked by the water's edge.

Suddenly, there was a big splash! Matt had fallen into the river!

"Hey, who's been chucking rubbish in here?" he shouted, pulling a pram out of the water.

The little lamb ran all the way back to Tom.

Fi thought it would help the little lamb to find her mummy if Tom stayed with her, and the other sheep, in the field.

Tom wasn't very happy with this idea. He had lots of work to do on the farm.

"I think you make a wonderful mummy," said Matt, smiling.

Meanwhile, naughty Buzz and Rev decided to have another race. They flew out of the farmyard and through the field.

They went so fast they scared the little lamb, who fell into the river! Tom rushed to save her.

Tom bravely drove further into the river to stop
the little lamb from being swept away. The water
in the river washed off all the honey and flour.
Tom was no longer white.

Back in the field the lamb
looked at Tom, but now
she didn't think he was
her mummy.
    "Ma-ma!" she called.
And ran over to the other sheep.

"I've got an idea," said Matt. And he went to get the pram he had found in the river.

He put one of the sheep inside the pram and the little lamb ran up to it calling, "Ma-ma!"

"Well done, Matt," said Fi. "The lamb thought that Tom was her mum when he looked like a sheep and now this sheep looks a bit like Tractor Tom!"

Back at the farmyard Fi and Matt cleaned and polished Tom.

"I'm glad we got that lamb sorted out," said Matt. "You know how sheep can be once they get an idea into their heads."

"Oh, no! Look!" shouted Fi. All the sheep had pram wheels and were racing down the hill. "They all want to be tractor-sheep!" laughed Fi!

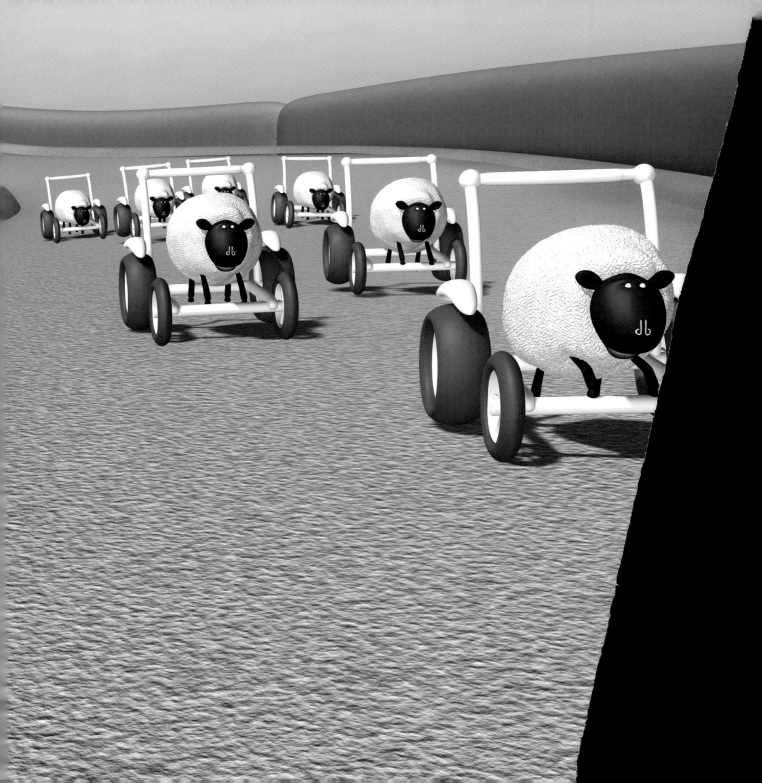

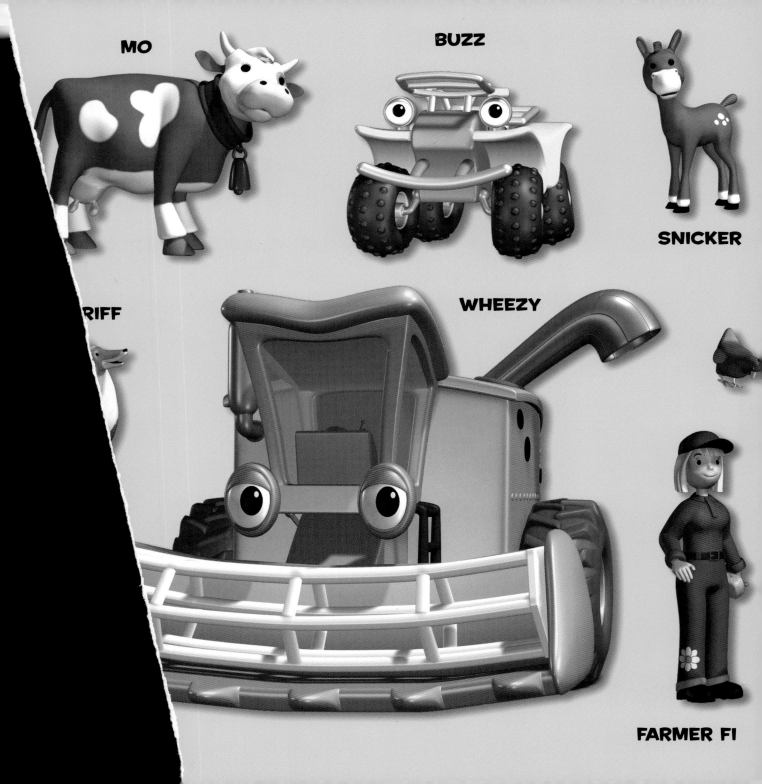

MO

BUZZ

SNICKER

RIFF

WHEEZY

FARMER FI

THE SHEEP

WACK

BACH

THE HENS

PURDEY

REV

TOM

WINNIE

MATT

YOU CAN COLLECT THEM ALL!

WWW.TRACTORTOM.COM

1-84357-066-1 £3.99 — TRACTOR TOM'S ACTIVITY BOOK

1-84357-064-5 £3.99 — TRACTOR TOM AND THE MOBILE PHONE

1-84357-065-3 £3.99 — TRACTOR TOM'S "WHERE'S IT GONE?" STICKER BOOK

1-84357-087-4 £3.99 — TRACTOR TOM'S SPORTS DAY

0-00-718904-4 £5.99 — MY TRACTOR TOM PLAYBOOK — FIND AND FIT THE SHAPES TO HELP TRACTOR TOM ON THE FARM!

0-00-718900-1 £3.99 — TREASURE TRAIL — COME TO THE BONFIRE PARTY WITH TRACTOR TOM!

0-00-718901-X £3.99 — A SURPRISE FOR FI — IT'S FI'S BIRTHDAY! CELEBRATE WITH TOM AND FRIENDS!

0-00-718902-8 £3.99 — BAA BAA TOM SHEEP — A LITTLE LAMB IS CAUSING PROBLEMS FOR TOM!

0-00-718903-6 £3.99 — A JOB FOR BUZZ — CAN TOM BE FIXED IN TIME TO SAVE THE DAY?

TRACTOR TOM™

WHAT WOULD WE DO WITHOUT HIM?